DO NOT READ THIS BOOK AT BEDTIME

by Bart King

art by Jacob Wenzka

c. 2018 New Growth Publishing

ISBN 978-0-9980832-2-3

NEW GROWTH PUBLISHING

Warning:

Do NOT read this book
at bedtime.

It will NOT
make you sleepy.

This book won't mention
how worn out you are
after a long day.

It won't mention
how tired your legs feel,
as if you snowshoed
to the South Pole
to build a snowman
with a colony of penguins.

It won't mention
how heavy your arms feel,
as if you swam
to the bottom of the ocean
to play school with the fish.

And it absolutely won't say
how good it feels
just to lie still in bed
after such a big day
exploring your world.

(You really do deserve a rest.)

This book won't
lull you to sleep
with soothing sounds
that feel good in your ears
but don't really mean much. Like...

Moonberry blossoms bloom in July.

June is for boomerangs boomering by.

Maybe the baby will sing lullabies.

Home again, home again ladybug fly.

Still awake? Good.

This book won't
draw attention to your eyelids,
even if they sink lower and lower.

Surely it's difficult to keep them open,
when the sun, too,
is going down for the night.

This book won't ask you
to just close your eyes
and think of something nice,
like dandelions.

You know, those white puff balls
that sometimes grow in the yard
on warm summer days.

With your eyes closed,
don't try to imagine
what it looks like
to blow those dandelions
into the breeze.

How lovely they look
heading off across the neighborhood.

Don't think about the smell
of grilled hot dogs in the air
and the laughter of friends
playing a game.

And don't focus on just one detail.
Don't forget about everything else,
even if you happen to notice
a tiny man, wearing a tiny hat,
drift happily by
holding onto a dandelion seed
like an umbrella.

The *last* thing this book would do
is teach you a secret way
to fall asleep.

It's a secret that has no pictures,
because it only works
if you close your eyes.
(Go ahead, give it a try.
We won't tell anyone.)

Now, lie very still
and pay close attention to your breath.
Notice how it feels
coming in through your nose
and then back out.

Notice how each breath
makes your belly inflate
like a balloon
and then shrink again.

In and out,
over and over,
each breath
makes you lighter and lighter,
until you float softly into dreamland.

Are you ready?
(If so, just nod your head.)

Now, breathe in, and out.
In
and out.
Notice that your feet
feel loose and light.

Breathe in, and out.
Feel your legs
floating weightless
on the bed.

Breathe in, and out.
Feel your belly,
light as air.

Breathe in, and out.
Your hands
are already asleep.

Breathe in, and out.
Your arms
are far away.

Breathe in, and out.
Your shoulders
are relaxed.

Breathe in, and out.
Your face
is soft and still.

Breathe in, and out.
And just let go.
What's left is perfectly you.

Breathe in, and float.
Have sweet dreams
until you wake
in the morning.

This is the third children's book collaboration by Bart King and Jacob Wenzka. The creative duo previously published 'The Girl Who Kept Night In Her Closet' (2017) and 'Juniper Gets Wet' (2015).

Bart makes his living as a communications consultant. When not taking care of clients or his young daughter, he can usually be found tending to the plants in his backyard or taking long walks around the neighborhood. He lives in Athens, Georgia.

Jacob is a painter and illustrator who lives with his wife and two children in Athens, Georgia. He works out of a messy basement studio where he sketches out his ideas on the concrete floor. He enjoys taking breaks from his painting to bang on the drums.

CPSIA information can be obtained
at www.ICGtesting.com
Printed in the USA
BVHW021332301118
534439BV00005B/11/P